BEING THE Best Me!

Dream On!
A book about possibilities

Cheri J. Meiners

★

illustrated by Elizabeth Allen

free spirit
PUBLISHING®

D0479766

Text copyright © 2016 by Cheri J. Meiners, M.Ed.
Illustrations copyright © 2016 by Free Spirit Publishing Inc.

Library of Congress Cataloging-in-Publication Data
Meiners, Cheri J., 1957–
      Dream on! : a book about possibilities / Cheri J. Meiners ; illustrated by Elizabeth Allen.
            pages cm. — (Being the best me series)
      Summary: "Helps children strengthen their imaginations, think about the future, and work toward goals. Back matter includes advice for motivating children and teaching about goal setting" — Provided by publisher.
            ISBN 978-1-63198-055-8
1. Achievement motivation—Juvenile literature. 2. Goal (Psychology)—Juvenile literature. I. Allen, Elizabeth (Illustrator) illustrator. II. Title.
      BF504.3.M45 2015
      155.4'138—dc23
                                                                                            2015014173

Reading Level Grade 2; Interest Level Ages 4–8;
Fountas & Pinnell Guided Reading Level K

Cover and interior design by Tasha Kenyon and Janet LaMere
Edited by Alison Behnke

10 9 8 7 6 5 4 3 2 1
Printed in China
R18860715

Free Spirit Publishing Inc.
217 Fifth Avenue North, Suite 200
Minneapolis, MN 55401-1299
(612) 338-2068
help4kids@freespirit.com
www.freespirit.com

In memory of my father, Victor,
for his dreams and his brilliant
design contributions to over
70 space missions

In my mind, anything is possible.
I can think and dream and imagine.

2

I have ideas and dreams for the future.
I believe that good things can happen,
and I hope they will.

Some of my dreams start now.

I take time to appreciate people
and enjoy what I already have.

I like to explore new ideas.

6

I'm finding out what I love to do
and where my dreams might take me.

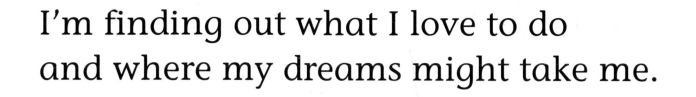

If I learn all about my dream,
and I imagine myself living it,
it starts to feel more real.

planets
Jupiter
Venus
Saturn
Earth
Mercury

When I see a dream clearly,

I picture in my mind what I want to happen, and I look forward to it.

I like to focus on ideas and goals that interest me.

I dream of exciting possibilities,
and what I might do someday.

13

It can take time and hard work for dreams to come true.

Things won't always happen the way I would like.
I may not do well at everything I try.

And some dreams
may depend on others.

Even when things don't go my way,
I can be patient and kind.

I can be happy for other people
when their dreams work out.

Things often turn out the way I hope.

And sometimes, things go even better than I expect!

It's exciting to know and learn about other people who follow their dreams.

23

I'm also grateful
for people who encourage me
to chase my dreams.

One of my dreams is to make a difference for someone else.

I like to help people I know,
and people I don't know.

27

It feels good
to be part of something
bigger than myself.

I have hope for the future.

I can do something each day to follow my dreams and be the best me.

Ways to Reinforce the Ideas in *Dream On!*

Dream On! teaches about imagination, goal setting, and problem solving. Young children who think about their dreams and their future are more prepared to cope with problems and are more likely to get along with others and be high achievers. As children incorporate some of the principles learned in the book, they may take on more responsibility for their own goals and view things through a more hopeful lens. In addition, the activities on pages 33–35 can motivate children to look forward to accomplishing difficult things. Here is a quick summary of key skills for imagination and goal setting, most of which are mentioned in the children's text:

1. Play and use your imagination. This can be a starting point for making dreams a reality.

2. Choose a dream that feels important to you.

3. Enjoy the dreams you are living today and the things that are happening right now.

4. Explore and learn about things you like, and be open to new things, too.

5. Imagine activities you'd like to take part in.

6. Picture yourself living a goal.

7. Work to make your dream happen.

8. Keep trying when things are hard.

9. Be inspired by other people's dreams.

10. Be a part of something that is bigger than you are.

Words to know:

Here are terms you may want to discuss.

appreciate: to enjoy, to be grateful, or to be thankful; to understand that something is important or good

dream: a wonderful idea, goal, or possibility

encourage: to help and reassure someone

expect: to look forward to; to think that something can happen

explore: to think about or learn about an idea or subject

focus: to pay close attention to something; to pay attention

future: time that is to come after today, like tomorrow, next year, or many years from now

grateful: appreciative or thankful; when you are grateful, you appreciate something and are glad for it

hope: the feeling that things will be okay or that good things will happen

imagine: to have a picture in your mind about something

As you read each spread, ask children:

- What is happening in this picture?

- What is the main idea?

- How would you feel if you were this person?

Here are additional questions you might discuss:

Pages 1–5

- What is something that you like to imagine when you play?

- How is a dream of something you want different from a dream you have at night?

- What do you hope will happen in the future for yourself? What about for someone you know?

- What is something you enjoy and appreciate right now?

Pages 6–15

- What is something you are good at? What do you love to do?

- What are things you want to learn more about? What new ideas do you want to explore?

- What is a dream that you can imagine living? What do you think it will feel like when your dream happens?

- What is something important that you want to do even if it seems hard?

- How can focusing on a dream or goal help it happen?

Pages 16–21
- What is a wish you have that could depend on someone else?

- How can being patient help when things don't go your way? How can being kind help?

- How can you show your support for others when their dreams work out?

- What is a time when something good happened, even if it wasn't what you expected or hoped for? How can you look for the good in situations that are disappointing at first?

Pages 22–31
- Who do you know who has followed a dream? What can you learn from this person?

- Who has encouraged you in a dream you have? What was your dream? How did the person help you?

- How can helping someone make a difference to the person? What is something you would like to do for someone else?

- What does it mean to "be part of something bigger than yourself"? Do you think that's a good idea? Why?

- How can being your best help you? How can it help someone else?

- Why do you have hope for your future? Why is it okay if you're not the best at everything? What is something you can do each day to be your best?

Games and Activities for Imagining Possibilities

Read this book often with your child or group of children. Once children are familiar with the book, refer to it as a tool to encourage imagination and goal setting, as well as to help children learn to handle the difficult emotions they may feel when their expectations or dreams don't become reality. In addition, use the following activities to reinforce children's understanding of how to develop and pursue their hopes and dreams.

Note: *Before beginning the activities, prepare the following cards and photographs to use with your group.*

Dream Cards

On individual 3" x 5" cards, write questions and prompts such as the following and others of your own. Make as many cards as you wish and plan to use your set of sample cards in the activities that follow.

- What is something you wish for?

- If you could go anywhere tomorrow, where would you go?

- If you could do something nice for somebody else, what would you do?

- What is something you would like to do when you are older?

- What is your biggest dream?

- Name something that you are good at.

- What is something about your life that makes you happy right now?

- When you play, what do you like to imagine?

- What is something you would like to be better at?

- If you could do anything you wanted to do all day, what would you do?

- If you wanted to be like a superhero, a famous person, or someone else, who would you choose? Why?

- If you could make any wish and know that it would definitely come true, what would it be?

Photographs of Children

Take a picture of each child, and print out at least two pictures for each child to use in the activities that follow.

Light at the End of the Tunnel

Materials: A few large boxes of similar size; duct tape; flashlight

Preparation: Open up the boxes at both ends. Tape the flap edges together to extend their length.

Directions: Lay the boxes on the floor. Have a child stand, sit, kneel, or crouch at the destination end of the "tunnel" and shine the flashlight downward. Another child begins walking or crawling through the box from the other end, using the flashlight as a point of reference. When a child reaches the end, that child can high-five the child holding the flashlight, and then hold the light for the next child coming through. Continue until every child has had a turn. Discuss how the flashlight is like our dreams. Seeing the flashlight at the end of the tunnel helps the child move toward it, just as a clear picture in our mind of our dream gives us motivation and courage to move toward it. This physical activity may be used as a warm-up for other dream activities.

Reach for the Stars

Materials: Yellow construction paper; scissors; star stencil or template, about 6" across; a picture of each child; crayons, colored pencils, markers; glue stick or double-sided tape; hole punch, yarn, and clothes hanger (for Variation)

Directions: Help each child trace a star shape on construction paper, using the stencil. (You can do this step ahead of time for younger children.) Crop each child's photo to a square about 3" by 3" and allow children to glue or tape their photos to their stars (helping if necessary). With the group, discuss how "reaching for the stars" is like trying to do something that seems hard or far away. Discuss goals that children might have for the coming weeks or months. Ask each child to choose a dream or goal to work toward or reach for. Help children write or draw pictures of these dreams on their stars' backs, and post children's stars on a bulletin board or in another prominent place. You can use this display to remind children of dreams they have and goals they are working on.

Variation: Punch a hole in each star and thread yarn through the hole. Attach stars to a hanger to make a mobile, or hang them directly from the ceiling using tape.

Dream Collage

Materials: Magazines and other sources of images; scissors; poster paper; glue sticks; a picture of each child (optional)

Level 1

Read aloud a selection of the Dream Cards (from page 33) as starting points for reflection and inspiration. Then allow children to each choose one question to focus on. Provide children with a variety of magazines and other sources of images that they can cut out. Encourage them to find illustrations and photos that appeal to them and that in some way represent their responses to the questions they chose. Help children cut out images if they need assistance.

Invite children to choose pictures that represent them in some way, or to use pictures of themselves, and to place these images in the center (or in some other prominent place) of their poster paper. Children can then arrange the rest of their chosen images on the paper however they like and glue them down to form a collage.

Level 2

Allow children time to share their collages with you or with the group, explaining what the pictures represent to them, and how they inspire the child to follow a goal or dream. Display the posters in a prominent place where they can be a reminder to children to focus on their dreams and hopes. You may want to give this display a heading such as "Our Dreams."

"Dream On" Book

Materials: Binder; plain sheets of 8½" x 11" paper; pencils, crayons, markers; note cards (for Level 2); shoe box or other container (for Variation)

Level 1

Let a child draw one of the Dream Cards. Read the card aloud or have the child do so. Then discuss the topic as a group, inviting children to draw pictures illustrating their responses to the card or depicting their dreams. Help each child write about his or her dream at the bottom or back of the picture. You can do this activity multiple times, using a different Dream Card each time. Add these pages to the binder to create a "Dream On" book for your group, and put the book in a place where children can access it. If you're in a school setting, consider making copies of children's responses to share with parents and caregivers.

Level 2

Hold "Dream On" interviews. In a one-on-one setting, read several Dream Cards to a child. Write down the child's responses as you discuss them. Take care not to discourage any dreams, even if they seem unattainable. Encourage the child to choose one realistic dream to focus on, and have the child decide on a plan or path to achieving that dream, offering your guidance as needed. Give the child a note card stating the goal or dream as a reminder. For younger children, you might also include a picture or symbol to represent their goal.

Variation: Rather than collecting children's papers in a binder, make a time capsule. Place papers in a shoe box or similar container. Mark the box with a date to be opened in the future—such as one month, six months, or one year. At the appointed time, the whole group could open the time capsule and review the contents to reflect on change, progress, and new or revised dreams.

Dreaming of New Solutions

Materials: Pictures of items like furniture, appliances, electronics, vehicles, and toys; card stock or index cards

Preparation: Make "Item Cards" by gathering the item images and mounting each picture to a piece of card stock or an index card.

Discussion: Let a child draw an Item Card. Ask what the item is and what it does or how it is used. Let children brainstorm and imagine something else that the object might do, or a way it could be improved. Explain that many of the recent innovations we have are a reality because people dreamed that it would be possible to do or make something—before it ever existed—and then worked hard to create it.

A Whole World of Dreams

Materials: Photographs of children

Discussion: Using pictures of the children (from page 33), show one photo at a time. Ask the group to name the child and some of his or her positive characteristics and achievements. Then ask children to brainstorm positive things that they can imagine this child doing in the future. Ideas could include academic, artistic, or sports achievements; service and volunteering actions; innovations; future careers; family life; or whatever else they imagine. The purpose of the exercise is to widen children's view of their own potential and possibilities, and to give them new ideas for their dreams, as well as to see potential in others.

Dream for a Friend

Discussion: Many stories, fairy tales, and fables are built on dreams coming true. The fulfilling of dreams doesn't truly depend on magic, however. It usually depends on hard work. Help from others is often important, as well. Choose a tale with a dream or hope at its center (such as the story of Aladdin, Pinocchio, or Cinderella), and use it as a springboard for talking about how children can achieve their dreams in real life. Also discuss traditions that exist for making wishes, and choose one to simulate. For instance, children might think of their dreams while pretending to blow out candles on a birthday cake, watching a shooting star, or throwing a coin in a fountain.

Place children in pairs. Have children tell their partners dreams that they are willing to share. Have children discuss together how they might help each other reach their dreams and goals. Guide them to ask and answer questions such as the following: "What would you do if your dream came true? How would you feel?" "What is something you can do to reach your dream?" "How could I help you?" "If your dream didn't come true for a long time, what else could you do?" Talk about ways that children can continue to encourage their partners.

Get the Whole Being the Best Me! Series
by Cheri J. Meiners

Books that help young children develop character traits and attitudes that strengthen self-confidence, resilience, decision-making, and a sense of purpose.

Each book: 40 pp., color illust., PB,
11¼" x 9¼", ages 4–8.

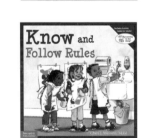